DREAMINGWITH
FROST

A DISTANT DREAMS & CRYSTAL FROST NOVELLA
ALICIA RADES

Published by Crystallite Publishing.

Produced in the United States of America.

Cover design by Desiree DeOrto and Alicia Rades.

ISBN: 978-0-9991872-3-4

To my fans who asked for more.

1

My lungs burned as I inhaled another deep breath. *Slow down*, my body demanded, but I didn't listen. The stomping of his feet grew louder. Any second now and he'd be able to reach out and grab me. I couldn't let him get that close. I pushed forward until I couldn't sprint any faster. I didn't think I would make it.

Just as I reached my max speed, I spotted the clearing. The grass ahead stood as a glimmer of hope. Just a couple of yards left. I increased my stride, hoping that would give me the extra boost I needed to make it there. Those last few steps seemed as long as the last mile I'd just run. Almost there… Finally, I broke through the trees and into the clearing. I did it!

I slowed. In my attempt to catch my breath, I couldn't manage to get the words out to gloat on my victory. Instead of saying anything, I shot my fists in the air and turned toward Collin with a grin on my face.

He gasped to catch his own breath, but after a moment, he managed to speak. "Congratulations, Kai."

Even though my victory meant he'd lost our race up the bluff, I knew his compliment was genuine. Ever since we'd started running together a month ago, I'd been getting better now that I had someone to challenge myself against. We were both going out for cross country next year, and I figured if we continued training together until next season, we'd both be good enough to make it to state.

Collin and I paced next to each other to cool down from our run.

I finally found my voice. "Thanks, but you let me win, didn't you?"

He shook his head. "I swear I didn't. You're getting faster."

I raised a brow. "Or maybe you're getting slower." My lips twitched in an attempt to hold back my teasing smile.

"Not a chance." He didn't even try to hide the amusement in his expression.

Neither of us said anything for another minute as our heart rates returned to normal. Collin leaned against the wooden barrier that was supposed to keep people from getting too close to the edge of the cliff. It didn't work. People climbed over and hung their feet off the edge or jumped into the water below all the time.

Luckily, no one had gotten hurt yet.

I joined him and rested my hip against one of the wooden posts, staring off into the distance. Just a month ago, I wouldn't have dared cross this barrier. Now I wasn't afraid, not with Collin by my side. Though he'd managed to ease some of my fears, I still couldn't get past the biggest one of all: telling him my secret. The thing was, I *wanted* to tell him. I just didn't think I could. No one would believe me, not Collin, not Savannah, not even my family. I'd known forever that my dreams were different than everyone else's, and because of that, I'd never told anyone about what I could do.

"What is it?" Collin asked. He took a step toward me until I could feel the heat from his body.

That was the first time I noticed the chilly evening air between us. Now that I was no longer moving, the November temperatures didn't seem as inviting. I was glad I wore long sleeves and my running pants. Even though I'd dressed for the weather, an involuntary shiver ran down my spine. I wasn't sure if it was because of the air or because of the question he'd just asked that I didn't want to answer.

"Nothing," I lied. A red strand of hair escaped my ponytail and flew in front of my face to the rhythm of the wind. I reflexively tucked it behind my ear without meeting Collin's eyes.

"Come on, Kai." He took another half-step toward me until the chilly air couldn't find its way between us anymore. His hands in mine warmed my skin. "You have to tell me eventually."

Finally, I looked him in the eyes. I did it mostly to assure him that nothing was bothering me, which was a total lie. "Tell you what?"

He squeezed my hands for encouragement. "Whatever it is that you keep thinking about. For the past week or so, you keep staring off into the distance like that, like something is on your mind."

I gulped down the lump that was beginning to form in my throat. *How did he catch on so easily? And what can I possibly say to him? Certainly not the truth. I'm not ready to be shipped off to a mental institution. He won't believe me.*

"It's nothing, really." My gaze shied away from his again, and I stared out past the edge of the cliff at nothing in particular.

"Kai, we may have not been dating long, but I think I know you better than you think I do. Don't you trust me?"

My muscles tensed, and I only hoped he didn't notice. His hands were still in mine, so I was guessing he felt the change in my body. I did trust him. I really did. I just didn't know if he would trust me, if he'd believe me. I wasn't willing to risk the humiliation of that scenario just yet. But I had to give him something...

"I do trust you," I told him quickly. "It's just...not something I'm ready to tell you yet." *There. That should satisfy him, right?*

"You can always talk to me." He leaned in even closer, and before I knew what was happening, his lips

4

brushed across mine.

The moment his lips were on mine, I thought I had satisfied his curiosity. But once he pulled away, my hopes were instantly crushed.

"So, what's wrong?" he asked kindly.

Could I do it? Could I tell him about my astral travels? Did I even want him to be the first to know? What about Savannah? If I told anyone, she'd be right at the top of the needs-to-know list. My heart pattered against the inside of my chest. *Nope. Now is definitely not the time to tell him my secret.*

"Collin, it's — I…" I licked my lips to stall. Another two seconds ticked by, and he was still eagerly waiting for my confession. *Just say something, Kai,* I demanded of myself. The words tumbled out of my mouth before I could snap my jaw shut. "I love you."

This time, I swore my heart stopped. I wasn't sure if that was better than the whole nervous hammering thing, but I knew it meant something. It was the first time I'd said it. Did I actually mean it? *Of course you meant it, you dummy!* I told myself. Still, I couldn't believe I'd actually said it. Out loud. I nervously glanced at him to assess his reaction.

Collin beamed, which sent my heart beating at its usual pace again. "I love you, too." He pulled me into an embrace, catching me slightly off guard. When he drew away, he spoke again. "That was all you were worried about? Telling me how you felt?" He reached up to brush my runaway strands of hair out of my face.

ALICIA RADES

"You don't ever have to worry about telling me how you feel, okay?"

I nodded without saying anything. At least I managed to get through the conversation without divulging my secret. But even as Collin walked me home, a sense of disappointment washed over me. Had I missed my chance to tell him about my gift? I wanted to tell him, but I wasn't sure how to explain it to him when I wasn't even sure of how it worked myself. I think that's what scared me the most.

2

Sleep had always come easily to me. It was the one thing I looked forward to throughout the day, but tonight, the darkness that was once inviting enveloped me uncomfortably. I lay awake, fully alert, with my eyes turned toward the ceiling.

I should put some glow-in-the-dark stars up there, I thought to myself absentmindedly. *Then at least I'd have something to stare at.*

Most nights weren't like this. I could usually fall asleep instantly, excited about where my astral travels would take me. Tonight, I only lay awake wondering about my ability and how I could possibly work up the courage to tell my family and friends about it.

I'd always known that my spirit left my body when I fell asleep. For the past four years, I knew that if I closed my eyes and envisioned a new location, I could transport my spirit there in a snap. I could conjure up my own images of my clothing or imagine the heat of the sun on my skin, and I could actually feel the sensation. It was like anyone else's dreams, only my spirit was in a real place, seeing the events as they happened.

Despite knowing all this, I figured there had to be more to my gift. Were there other people who could do what I did? Why me? Was I capable of more than just dreaming of real places? And what would happen when I finally told someone?

Ever since my gift returned a month ago—after a two-week period where my travels had been replaced by nightmares—I'd been contemplating all of this more and more. I'd never been that interested in learning about what I could do. I'd only ever wanted to use my gift to travel the world, to get away. But lately, curiosity had started to get to me. *Someone* else had to be out there, someone who could do what I could and teach me what I was capable of. Maybe if I knew more about it all, I could finally open up to the people I loved.

That's it. I pushed up from my bed and padded over to my laptop. A guilty sensation hit me in the gut as I opened my computer. My mom would have a fit if she knew I was up this late searching the Internet. After all, it was a school night, but I couldn't sleep with these thoughts racing around in my mind.

I started by typing a few keywords into the search

bar. I began with *astral travel*. I'd researched the term before when I was 12, and I'd come to the conclusion that that's what my gift really was, that I was projecting my spirit onto the astral plane. But I wasn't sure if it fit exactly. Some of my research said that people could travel through time to view past events while their spirit was out of their body. I certainly hadn't traveled through time. I also read that there were several different planes you could travel to, not just the astral plane, so which one was I traveling to? And wouldn't I have *seen* someone else by now if others could do this as well? Regardless, "astral travel" was the best word I had for it.

I pressed my lips together and narrowed my eyes at the screen. *Maybe I need to find one of these people who can do what I do and get them to answer my questions.*

My fingers hit against the keyboard ferociously. I quickly scanned the search results and found several forums detailing people's out of body experiences, but the problem was that I had no idea which ones were legit or not. I briefly considered signing up for the forum myself and posting my questions, but then I wondered about the legitimacy of the information I'd receive. I didn't need a group of random strangers telling me this and that. I needed a mentor, someone who legitimately knew about the paranormal. If I could talk with them over the phone, even better.

After reading through several forum posts, I headed back to the search page. For a moment, I just stared at the computer screen with my hands resting on the keyboard. Who could I possibly contact about my questions? What would they call themselves? A psychic, maybe? On and on, my search continued through psychic's blogs and phone psychic advertisements until I had the brilliant idea to narrow my search for geographical location. Could there be someone nearby who was like me?

I must have been sitting at the computer for two hours before I found a promising web page. My cheek rested in my hand, and my eyes began to droop. As soon as I started reading the page, I immediately perked up. My face drew closer to the computer screen as if magnetized while I read about a woman who had admitted to her entire town that she was psychic. The person who'd posted the comment seemed skeptical, but he talked about how the town always had their suspicions about the woman. She ran a psychic-themed shop, he said, called Divination, and her tarot card readings were so accurate that he accused her of cheating somehow. Could this woman possibly know something about the paranormal and help me out?

I quickly searched the town he was talking about. I'd never heard of Peyton Springs before, but as soon as the directions popped up, my fingers began to shake in excitement. It was a drive, but I could make a day trip out of it.

I returned to the tab that talked about the shop called Divination. My eyes narrowed at the screen.

Could this lady really know what she was talking about and help me understand my gift? There was only one way to find out.

***

"Why not?" I complained to my mother the following evening. "Why can't I have the car for just the day on Saturday?"

My mom let out a breath of air like she couldn't believe what I was asking. She turned to me after closing the dishwasher and pressing the start button. "Because I'm not comfortable with you driving alone yet. You haven't had your license that long, and in the time you have had it, you haven't gotten much practice."

That's because we never go anywhere together, I wanted to say, but I held my tongue. "But Mom, I'm a good driver."

She placed her hands on her hips and stared at me from across the kitchen. "What do you even need the car for?"

I shrugged, but inside, my blood was boiling. "I want to go shopping and stuff. You know? I just need a day to myself. I'll use my own money for gas."

My mother laughed. "It's not about the gas money, Kai. It's about your safety. I don't want you driving alone yet."

I crossed my arms over my chest. I couldn't believe how unfair she was being! Sure, things had been better between us lately, but she was still my mother and sometimes acted in ways I couldn't quite wrap my head around.

"What about if someone else comes with me?" I suggested, even though I wanted to go alone.

"You mean Savannah or Collin?" She turned to the sink to wet a washcloth.

It took me a second to realize my mouth was hanging open. "Uh, yeah."

She wiped down the counter as she spoke. "That's not any better than driving alone. You'll get distracted with your friends in the car."

"Then why can't I go alone? There won't be any distractions then."

"No," she said, her pitch rising.

"What if Savannah or Collin drove me?"

"Kai!" She threw down her rag, and I could swear her voice echoed off the kitchen walls. "I said no."

"But Mom—"

"End of discussion."

"But what if—"

"No. You're not ready to drive the car without me, and the more you push it, the less chance you have of me letting you go *anywhere* at all."

I was about to suggest that she come with me, but she didn't let me finish. It's not like I wanted her to come. I loved my mom, but I didn't think she'd be the first person I told about my gift.

Sometimes I wondered if my ability to step out of

my body at night was inherited from one of my parents. I could remember times when I was little, though, that my family talked about the weird dreams they'd had, and I knew I was somehow an anomaly. My dreams never felt as strange as my family described. It always felt *real*, just as real as it felt to stand in the kitchen and argue with my mother. I knew that if I tried to tell her about what I could do, she wouldn't believe me.

The couple of times I did mention what I'd done while sleeping—it was dumb things like watching cartoons or stalking the neighbor's cat—she would always reply with something like, "That's a silly dream, Kai." Of course, I was like six, which was right around the time when I started to realize no one else left their bodies when they slept.

When I returned to my room after the argument with my mother, I plopped down onto my bed angrily. If I couldn't go meet this psychic lady in person, then I'd have to come up with an alternative. *Maybe I could call her shop and talk to her. Maybe I should go join one of those forums. Or maybe . . .*

"Duh!" I said out loud, making me actually seem somewhat crazy for real. *I don't need a car to go somewhere! I can astral travel, and I can find her on my own.* Granted, I wasn't going to get any answers out of this lady since she wouldn't be able to see me, but at least I could scope the place out and see if it's even *worth* a drive over there.

It was still a few hours to bedtime, but I was eager

to learn more. I slipped into my pajamas and under my sheets and drifted off.

3

I relaxed until sleep overcame me. Once it did, my spirit stepped out of my body. I gazed down at my sleeping form. I looked so serene, so peaceful. The sounds of the TV in the living room reached my ears, pulling me to attention. I tore my gaze off my body and sighed. Braden's show wasn't going to make sleeping very easy. I already felt weak and groggy, an indication that I'd sleep lightly tonight. But I was too excited to wait for my body to fall deeper into sleep.

I closed my eyes and visualized the shop I'd seen online. When I opened them, I stood on a secluded sidewalk in a quiet town. The shop in front of me wasn't very big, but its sign and trinkets in the windows drew the eyes. I let out a disappointed sigh when I saw the lights were out and they were closed. It must have taken me longer to fall asleep than I thought. Still, curiosity got the better of me. I took a step toward the shop and peered in through the window. The street lamp next to me illuminated the front of the shop enough that I could make out the silhouettes of shelves and tables.

Stepping back from the window, I straightened my spine and took a deep breath. *Here goes nothing.* My feet moved forward, but I didn't feel the brick wall crash into me. Within three steps, I'd passed through the wall and stood inside the shop. A sense of guilt tingled throughout my body. It was almost like I was breaking and entering since they weren't open, but it wasn't like I was here to take anything; I just wanted to see if the place was worth making the drive for.

After another deep breath to calm my nerves, I stepped closer to one of the shelves to eye the products they had on display. Walking slowly through the shop, I inspected the areas that weren't cast in complete darkness. Magic kits, crystal balls, candles, dream catchers, and more lined the shelves. It all seemed too touristy to me, like it was all just for show. Could this lady be for real?

Eventually, I reached a stack of books. I skimmed over each title, and one of the words immediately caught my eye. *Dreams.* A book about dreams? Could it tell me more about what I can do? I wanted to reach out and grab the book, but I knew my fingers would only pass through it the same way my body had passed through the wall. I stared closer at the cover facing me and let out a disappointing sigh. It read, *Dreams: An Interpretation of Symbols*. It sounded more like it was about decoding your dreams than explaining my abilities.

I was about to turn away from the stack of books when a *thud* toward the back of the shop caught my attention. I tensed in surprise and instinctively crouched behind the display.

"Mom?" a female voice called out.

I relaxed slightly when I reminded myself no one could see me. Sometimes I forgot to sort my out of body experiences from my everyday encounters, but it was better to heed caution. Though no one could see me, that didn't keep me from inching slowly toward the sound of the voice like I thought I might get caught.

"Mom?" the girl called again.

A moment later, the hallway leading to the back of the shop became flooded in light. I peeked around the corner and spotted a thin blond girl who looked to be about my age standing in front of a doorway. Her hand rested on the doorknob to hold it open. The light in the room spilled out into the hallway.

"You didn't answer your cell," the girl said to someone inside the room.

"Sorry," a groggy female voice replied. "My phone must have died. These numbers weren't adding up, so Diane and I stayed back to see if we could figure out where the problem was."

"Where is she?" The girl with long blond hair

shifted in the doorway.

"She left a few minutes ago. I was just finishing up and then was going to come home."

"Okay. Teddy has food ready. You said you'd be home earlier, so I thought I'd come check on you."

The woman inside the room cleared her throat. "Give me a minute, and we'll walk home together, okay?"

The girl nodded.

I gritted my teeth from behind her. Why couldn't my mom be as nice as this girl's mom? She talked to her like she was her equal, not some kid who didn't understand what she was saying. Why was it so easy for some people and not for me? My eyes locked on the girl while she waited for her mother, so I noticed when her body tensed.

"Mom," she whispered.

I spotted her mother through the doorway. She had the same golden shade of hair as her daughter. She shot her a questioning expression.

"Do you feel that?" the girl whispered.

Her mother shook her head.

"Look." The girl used her left hand to point to her right arm, which still hung from the doorknob. "Goosebumps." Her voice came out so soft that I barely heard it.

I figured they must have some sort of inside joke that I was missing out on, and I felt like a creep for listening in to their conversation, not that the conversation was important. I straightened up, preparing to turn back to inspect the displays and leave the two women in privacy. Before I could turn away, though, the girl in the doorway swiveled in my direction.

And she stared directly at me.

My spirit sprang back into my body, and I bolted upright in bed. My chest compressed, and it took me a moment to realize I wasn't breathing. I forced air into my lungs and slowly lowered myself to my pillow. I pulled the covers up to my chin, but my eyes remained wide.

She saw me. What does that mean?

I swallowed deeply, but I still hadn't managed to blink. She looked right *at* me. Not *through* me. *At* me. How was that possible?

I didn't know, but I knew one thing for sure: I had to go back there in person and get some answers.

4

Mom wasn't going to let me make the drive myself. I maybe could have lived with her decision if it wasn't for what had happened while I was astral traveling. I *needed* to meet the blond girl who saw me and figure out *why*. Was it possible that she could astral travel, too? Was that why she saw me?

If only I'd caught her name and could find her online. I tried searching for girls about my age on Facebook, filtering by location. Peyton Springs wasn't any bigger than Amberg, so I didn't think it'd be too hard. Unfortunately, I didn't get a good look at her face. Without a name, it was even more difficult. That's why I needed to see her in person.

I didn't bother pushing Mom to let me go. I knew the more I asked, the less she'd be willing to let me do *anything* on my own. Instead, I asked her if I could stay the night at Savannah's over the weekend, and she reluctantly agreed.

"We're going on a road trip," I'd told Savannah bluntly, and her eyes lit up in response.

"I can't believe we're doing this," she told me Saturday morning while applying her makeup.

"I know. I just want to meet my friend in person, and Mom won't let me. Promise you won't say anything to your parents? I don't want them telling my mom."

Savannah ran two pinched fingers over her lips and threw the invisible key over her shoulder. "My lips are sealed. So, tell me more about this friend."

I fell to Savannah's bed and leaned against the canopy post. "It's just a girl I met online." It wasn't a complete lie, but what was I supposed to tell my best friend? That I saw the girl while I was dreaming? I wasn't ready for that, so I concocted a lie I knew she'd believe.

"And your mom won't let you go meet her? That's so unfair! It's not like you're going to meet up with a boy."

I sighed. It wasn't the worst thing I could do, but nervous butterflies still danced around in my stomach when I thought about how I was going against my mother's wishes.

Savannah gave a giggle from across the room. "I've never done anything rebellious before."

You wouldn't think that looking at her. This week,

her hair was the color of a ripe plum, and her eye makeup was so dark that it made her eyes look twice their size. A lip ring and nose piercing would have suited her ensemble well, but she said she had enough holes in her face with the double piercings in her ears.

"Yeah, well…" I couldn't manage to find the words to finish my sentence. *I'm not proud of it*, is what I wanted to say, but I didn't want Savannah to get suspicious of why I was doing this. I didn't care what my mom said, though. I *had* to find answers.

Savannah puckered her lips in the mirror one last time before standing from her chair. "Okay. Let me just grab my purse, and I'll be ready to go."

I slipped my own purse over my shoulder and followed Savannah down the hall. My breathing ceased, and my hands broke into a nervous sweat. *I have no idea what I'm doing*, I told myself repeatedly. What would happen once I got there? Would I even find the blond girl at Divination, and if I didn't, where would she be? How could I ask questions with Savannah around? Was there some way to distract her? I had several hours in the car to figure out a game plan, but that didn't seem like enough time. Heck, I was going to meet up with a girl who saw me *astral traveling*. There would never be enough time to prepare myself for this.

My purse buzzed against my hip as I clicked open Savannah's passenger side door. I slid into the seat and pulled my phone out of my purse. It was a text from Collin.

You up to anything today?

Crap! I thought. *What should I say?*

Just hanging with Savannah, I texted back with shaky fingers.

Oh, cool. I was bored. You two mind if I join?

"What's up?" Savannah asked, gesturing to my phone. She flipped her purple hair over her shoulder and clicked her seatbelt into place.

"It's just Collin. He wants to hang out." Normally, I wouldn't mind, but how could I keep them both occupied while I secretly talked to the blond girl about what I could do?

Savannah shrugged. "I don't mind if he comes along."

It took me a second to realize I was pursing my lips. I forced my face to relax. "No, he really doesn't have to—" I cut off as soon as I began formulating a counterargument. Maybe they could keep *each other* occupied so that I could have a few moments alone with the girl.

Apparently I'd remained silent for too long. Savannah stared at me with raised eyebrows. "Well, is he going to hang out with us or not? I gotta know where I'm headed."

I sighed. I only hoped I'd get some answers out of this trip. "Yeah, he can come. Let me check with him real quick."

We're headed out of town. You up for a road trip?

Five minutes later, Collin and I were seated

together in the back seat of Savannah's compact car, and I was giving her directions to Peyton Springs.

Please, God, I thought. *Don't let this be a mistake.*

5

Luckily, Savannah and Collin didn't ask too many questions on the way. I stuck to my story about meeting the girl online and told them I wanted to meet her because we shared mutual interests. That wasn't a lie — I hoped — but when they asked what I meant, I told them she was a runner like me. I hoped that was true. When they began asking more complicated questions — like what the girl's name was and why I hadn't mentioned her before — I dodged their questions by suggesting we listen to the radio. Savannah's voice rang above the music as she sang along, drowning out all conversation.

Twenty minutes from Peyton Springs, I released Collin's hand that had been entwined in mine the whole trip. I didn't want him to notice the way they began to increasingly sweat the closer we got.

What am I doing? I asked myself again. Though I'd had hours to formulate a plan, I hadn't managed to figure out anything beyond stepping into Divination and crossing my fingers. Hopefully the blond girl would be there. Hopefully Savannah and Collin would get distracted by the crystal balls or something. And hopefully I'd get some answers about my gift.

She has to know something, I told myself. *She saw me. No one's ever seen me outside of my body before.* I obsessed over this detail the whole ride there.

"What's with this place?" Savannah eyed the brick building as we drove up to it.

I shrugged, hoping it came across nonchalantly. "Her mom works here. You know, you guys don't have to come in. You could—" I paused for a moment before my voice cracked out of nerves. Hopefully neither of them noticed my hand shivering against the door handle. I forced myself to recover quickly. "You could go get coffee or something. I don't mind."

Savannah let out an amused breath of air. "It's no problem. This place looks interesting anyway." She stepped out of the vehicle.

Collin turned to me and spoke for the first time since Savannah had turned on the music. "Are you okay, Kai?"

I blinked far too rapidly for my own liking. "What? Yeah. I'm fine."

He was starting to get to know me too well, but he let the lie slide. He leaned over to give me a peck on the cheek before turning to his door and sliding out of the car. I followed my friends into the shop. The bell above the door rang, earning us a friendly smile from the woman behind the counter. She was tall and plump with a pile of auburn hair tied into a loose bun atop her head. I returned an attempted smile and proceeded to occupy my gaze with one of the candles nearby. Savannah sniffed one and let out a moan of pleasure.

"Well, are you going to find your friend?" Collin asked, shoving his hands in his jeans pockets and glancing around.

I had to release my lower lip from my teeth to answer. "Yeah. I just—um—wanted to look around a little."

He didn't question that and began inspecting the nearby dream catchers.

I glanced back up at the woman behind the counter. Nerves hit my gut so hard that a thin line of tears settled on my lower eyelid. *I can't do this*, I told myself. *I have no idea what I'm doing!* I literally didn't know what I was doing. My body moved on its own accord, and after a moment, I realized I'd made my way to the checkout counter. The woman behind it smiled at me.

"Can I help you find something?" she asked.

I couldn't meet her eyes. Instead, I stared at the array of chocolates in a display case next to her. It surprised me when a rumble came from my throat to clear it. Apparently my body was working on its own today. "What flavor do you recommend?" I managed to spit out.

"The truffles are one of our most popular. Are you a fan of peanut butter or mint? Those are my personal favorites."

"Mm…" I leaned toward the display case to inspect the flavors.

"Or perhaps strawberry?" the woman suggested. "You look like a strawberry kind of gal."

I laughed without having to force it. My fingers twirled around the end of my ponytail. "Is it the red hair?"

She visibly blushed. "Oh, no. I didn't mean—"

"It's okay. The strawberry chocolate sounds good." The tension in my shoulders eased when she shot me another smile. "I am actually looking for someone. Maybe you can help me?"

She pressed her lips together. "That depends on who you're looking for."

How could I even begin to describe her? *She's blond. About my age. Can see people who are astral traveling. Sound like anyone you know?*

"Her mom works here," was the best I could come up with.

"Oh." The woman stretched out the word in realization. "You mean Crystal."

Yes! I finally had a name for her.

"She doesn't come into the shop much anymore. She used to work here part-time, but then volleyball started, and of course, she wanted to spend time with

Robin, and she just got too busy." The woman waved her hand like I should know what she meant by all of that. "I'm Diane, by the way." Again, she said it like I should know who she was. Maybe if I actually knew Crystal, I would have heard of her. "Did you want me to ring up your total now, or should I hang onto these while you finish browsing?"

I glanced around the store. Savannah and Collin chatted near the magic kits, and I was suddenly glad I brought them both along so they could occupy each other. I turned back to the woman. "I'm not sure how long we're staying. So, Crystal isn't going to be around today?" I did my best to make it sound like we were friends.

Diane shook her head apologetically.

"It's just that I got a new phone, and I lost all my contacts. I was really hoping to talk to her." I silently applauded myself for how quick I was on my feet. *I should be, like, a professional liar*, I told myself, though I didn't think that was exactly something to be proud of.

"Well, she's probably at home. Or if you're in contact with Emma or Derek, you could ask one of them for her number."

I had no idea who these people were, but I tried my best to play along. "Like I said, I lost all my contacts. It's no big deal. I'll just—" I honestly didn't know how I was going to finish that sentence, but luckily the bell on the door rang just then, distracting us both.

Diane's gaze locked across the shop the same time

I turned to look at the person who'd just entered. Once I processed the long blond hair and thin frame, my heart stopped.

Crystal froze in the doorway, and the paper bag she held in her hand crashed to the floor.

6

It felt like time froze in the following moment as we stared at each other, but it couldn't have been more than a second before Crystal bent to scoop up her bag. She approached me without ever taking her eyes off mine. She opened her mouth twice to say something but closed it both times before getting anything out. Finally, she managed to tear her gaze off my face and look at Diane.

"My mom?" was all she said.

Diane gestured over her shoulder. "She's going through some inventory in the storage room."

Crystal held up the paper bag in her hand. "I didn't want her to go hungry. She keeps forgetting to eat, and she can't keep doing that. I—um—I'll go find her." Crystal surprised me by turning my way. "We need to talk."

My feet moved under me without consciously deciding to, and I followed her down the hall I'd seen her in the other night. I peeked back at my friends and saw they were now occupied by the crystal balls on display.

Crystal paused outside a door and peeked inside. "Mom, I brought you some lunch. I'll set it in the break room, okay? Don't forget it this time."

I couldn't see into the room, but I heard her mother's reply. "Thanks, sweetie."

Crystal crossed the hall and slipped her mother's lunch into another nearby room. The look she shot me told me to follow her. We continued to the end of the hall, out a door, and down a few steps into the chilly November air. At least the sun was out today, which helped warm my cheeks.

As soon as the door clicked shut behind us, we both spoke at the same time.

"Who are you?" Crystal asked.

"Can you astral travel?" I spoke simultaneously.

We both went silent for a moment in confusion.

Crystal was the first to speak. "What's going on? You're not..." She reached over to run her fingers across the back of my hand. It was awkward for a moment, but she came across friendly. "You're here...I mean, you're solid. You're not dead."

I nearly took a step away from her. "What? Um, no. Don't you know what I can do? That's why I came here.

I thought you knew something I didn't."

She tilted her head and spoke slowly. "I think we should start over. I'm Crystal." She reached her hand out in a friendly gesture. I had no other choice but to shake it.

I coughed to clear my throat. "I'm Kai."

She glanced down the street. When she saw no one else was around, she spoke slowly. "I'm only telling you this because there's clearly something going on here, but I'm…well…psychic. I see ghosts and predict the future." She crossed her arms over her chest. "And clearly you're not a ghost, so your turn."

Was she for real? Ghosts? Predicting the future? It sounded like she belonged in a mental institution. Except, wasn't that the exact reason I was too afraid to tell anyone about what I could do? If astral traveling was possible, wasn't all this other paranormal stuff just as likely to be real, too?

Apparently I hadn't said anything for a while because Crystal raised her eyebrows impatiently.

I cleared my throat again, but my voice still came out sounding small. "I'm, uh, not psychic. I…" My face grew hot despite the cool air brushing across it. I'd never said the words out loud before. I didn't even keep a diary where I could dish my secrets. It felt wrong to tell a complete stranger.

Crystal's shoulder's relaxed, and a compassionate expression crossed her face. "You've never told anyone, have you?"

A nervous giggle bubbled up from my throat, and I had to blink to keep the tears at bay. I crossed my arms over my chest and silently blamed the water in my eyes on the cold. "Is that a psychic thing?" I stared down the street at a naked tree while I spoke.

Crystal raised a single shoulder and then let it drop. "Not really, but I can feel other people's emotions when I touch them."

My eyes snapped back to hers. I couldn't believe what I was hearing. Ghosts. The future. Emotions. It all sounded so unbelievable, but at the same time, it amazed me. "So, when you touched me just now…?"

Crystal nodded. "I didn't mean to. I was just making sure you were real." She laughed lightly. "I don't get it, though. I saw you. I thought you were a ghost. It really kind of freaked me out when I saw you in there just now, all solid and everything."

"Honestly, I don't understand it myself." My knees began to shake uncontrollably, and it wasn't even that freezing outside. "Can we sit?"

I didn't wait for an answer. I sank onto one of the steps we'd just walked down. Crystal sat beside me. I didn't know what it was about her, but she seemed nice, like we could actually be friends.

It took me several seconds before I composed myself enough to speak again. I didn't like the idea of opening up so much to a stranger, but it was the reason I came. Plus, she'd just told me something personal without hesitation. Didn't I owe it to her to explain myself?

Once I started speaking, the words just sort of tumbled out of me. "I actually came to ask you about what I can do. Well, I mean, I came to ask the ladies in there." I gestured to the door behind me. "I don't know if it was your mom or the lady at the counter, but I read online about this woman who runs this shop. I thought that maybe she could tell me a little about the paranormal. When my mom wouldn't let me come, I decided to scope out the place and see if it was worth coming to. And that's when you saw me." I knotted my sleeve in my hands, but nothing I could do in this moment could slow my racing heart. Still, I knew I came here to tell someone, so I forced myself to spit it out. "The thing is, I don't really know much about it. That's why I'm looking for someone to help me. All I know is that when I fall asleep, my spirit leaves my body. I can take it anywhere I want. I just can't touch anything, and no one else can see me. Except for you." I began to relax the more I talked to her.

Crystal nodded like she understood. "It sounds a lot like astral traveling."

"That's what I thought!" My voice came out high and squeaky. Hope filled my heart. So she *did* understand, on some level at least. That made me feel a little better about telling a complete stranger my secret. "I mean, I don't know a lot about this stuff, so I'm just getting that from what I read online."

"You know what?" she asked kindly. "Maybe you

should talk to my mom. After all, she's the person you came here to talk to. My friend Emma is pretty good with this stuff, too." Crystal began to stand, but I stopped her.

"Your friends know? Like, that you're…" The word sounded strange on my tongue. The only concept of the paranormal I ever really considered was astral traveling. It sounded silly to think that all this other stuff Crystal said she could do was possible. "Psychic," I finished.

She nodded confidently.

"Oh. I—uh—my friends have no idea. The other two people in there? The guy is my boyfriend, and the girl is my best friend. I only brought them along for the ride."

She looked at me sympathetically. "You should tell them. I'm sure they'll be really understanding."

I crinkled my nose. "I don't know. We've never even *talked* about the supernatural. Up until a minute ago, I'd never told anyone in my life. You're the only person who knows what I can do. And I only told you because I thought maybe you could help me understand it. And, well…you seem nice."

"Thanks," she said with a smile. "But they're your best friends. I'm sure they'll support you."

"I don't think I'm ready for that."

That expression of understanding crossed her face again, and I mentally thanked her for not pushing it any further. Wait. Could she read my thoughts? With the way she looked at me, it didn't appear that was how it worked. Thank God.

"I should get back to my friends, though," I told her. "I kind of just disappeared on them. I'd like to talk to your mom, though, if she knows anything."

We both stood. Crystal reached for the handle on the door, but before she could pull it open, I grabbed her wrist to stop her.

"Wait! My friends think we know each other. I told them we met online and that I wanted to meet you because we're both into running. I hope you like to run."

A wide smile spread across her face. "Running isn't my thing, but I can play along. Anything else I should know?"

I relaxed my grip on her wrist and felt the tension in my body ease. I got lucky that she was so nice. "I don't think so."

7

By the time I returned to the front of the shop, Savannah and Collin had made it back to the candles and were sniffing them again. They both looked up when they noticed my approach.

"Hey, guys. This is my friend I was telling you about. Crystal, these are my friends." Thankfully, my voice came out sounding stronger than it had all day.

"Hi." Savannah gave a light wave. "Kai didn't tell us much about you. We were starting to wonder if you were real."

Leave it to Savannah and her big mouth to make the conversation awkward. I didn't miss when Collin lightly elbowed her in the ribs. She shot him the evil eye.

"It's great to meet you," Collin said sweetly, reaching out to shake Crystal's hand.

"You, too," Crystal replied, moving to shake Savannah's hand as well. "Kai's told me so much about you." Her eyebrow twitched ever so slightly at the lie, but neither Collin nor Savannah seemed to notice. "It's so great to meet you all in person."

Collin shoved his hands in his pockets. "Well, now that we're all here, was there a plan? Are we hanging out here the rest of the day?"

That was my problem. I didn't really have a plan. I subtly bumped my arm up against Crystal's. She said she could read emotions by touching people. I hoped she would hear my silent plea for help. I wasn't sure if it was her psychic powers or just the tension in the air, but she responded quickly.

"Would it be weird if I invited you to my house?"

Savannah and Collin exchanged a glance.

"That sounds fine," Collin said. "I mean, Kai knows you, so if she's fine with it, so are we."

"Great." Crystal smiled. "Let me just go talk with my mom." She disappeared into the hallway again.

"She seems nice." Collin moved to entwine his fingers in mine. The gesture relaxed the final bit of my lingering nerves.

"Yeah," Savannah agreed, setting down the last candle she'd sniffed. "I like her."

"Thanks, guys. Hey! Does anyone want chocolates? I'll buy," I offered.

My friends and I approached the counter where Diane had kept my chocolates safe for me. Collin and

Savannah picked out their own candies, which she added to the bag. Just as Diane handed over the receipt, Crystal emerged from the hallway.

"My mom says you guys can come over. You ready?"

***

Crystal took the front seat in Savannah's car and gave her directions to her house. As strange as it may seem to be invited over to a complete stranger's house, this didn't feel that weird.

"Feel free to take off your shoes and get comfortable," Crystal offered when we entered her living room. "Anyone want some snacks? Maybe lunch? Kai, can you help me in the kitchen?"

Her kitchen was mostly open to her living room, but there was a short wall separating part of it that gave us a small amount of privacy.

She pressed her hands to her face for a moment before dropping them. "I'm sorry if this is weird. I think we need some more time to talk about things, and I needed to distract your friends. I sent my friends a 911 text, so they'll be coming over soon. This was the only place I thought we could all go. There's not exactly much to do in this town."

I knew exactly what she meant. There wasn't anything to do in Amberg, either. "It's fine, really. Just as long as your parents don't mind." *And mine will never know,* I thought.

"Yeah, it's fine. I convinced my mom. Remember how I can feel people's emotions? Well, it was pretty clear when I touched each of you that you're all trustworthy."

I smiled at that. *So the handshake thing was a ploy. Very sneaky, Crystal. I like you.*

"Snacks?" Crystal turned to the cupboard.

We returned to the living room with a bag of pretzels and some string cheese.

"Sorry, guys," Crystal said. "This is all we have for snacks."

Savannah straightened up on the couch. She'd already stripped her shoes off. "Oh, that's so nice of you! It's totally fine. I'm just hungry." She took a string cheese from Crystal's outstretched hand.

"Thank you," Collin said from the couch when Crystal handed him the pretzels.

The doorbell rang, and Crystal hurried over to answer it. I took a seat between my friends and leaned into Collin's shoulder. It was warm and inviting.

An excited female voice came from just outside the door. "I brought games!"

"We have *more* than enough," a male voice agreed.

Crystal opened the door wider to invite her friends inside.

"Hi," the girl sang cheerfully as she set her pile of board games on the ground. The boy placed an equally high stack next to it.

"These are my friends Emma and Derek," Crystal introduced. "And this is my friend Kai and her friends Savannah and Collin."

We all exchanged nervous smiles and waves.

Emma brushed dark curly hair out of her face and then held onto Derek's hand. Apparently they were an item. "So, what do you guys want to play first?" she asked.

Savannah hurried over to the pile of games to inspect which ones Emma had brought along. Meanwhile, Collin wrapped an arm around my waist and pulled me close, placing a light kiss along my hairline.

"You okay?" he asked.

I tore my gaze from the amusing show of excitement Savannah was putting on. "Yeah, I'm fine. Why?"

"You've seemed nervous all day."

I squirmed slightly. How had we only been going out a month and he already knew me so well? "It's just this whole meeting new people thing. I'm not that good with people."

"I noticed," he said.

"What?" I practically squeaked. I hadn't expected him to agree with me.

Only a second later did a hint of a smile touch his lips. I poked at him playfully.

"*Sorry*! I love this game!" Savannah exclaimed, holding the box out in front of her. "Too bad it's only for four players."

"That's perfect!" Crystal said from across the room with almost too much enthusiasm. "I mean, that's fine. Kai and I have some catching up to do anyway. We don't mind." I caught her exchange a glance with Emma.

"That's great!" Emma reached for the box in Savannah's hand. "I love this game, too. Now we have the perfect amount of players." I suspected she was playing off whatever look it was Crystal shot her way to earn us some privacy.

"You go play," I told Collin. "I don't mind."

"You're just going to leave Savannah and me here with strangers?" he asked in a whisper.

I glanced over at Savannah. She was the most outgoing person I knew, so I knew she wouldn't mind making new friends. But Collin was a different story.

"I want to get to know Crystal a little more," I told him, almost pleading.

After a long pause, he sighed heavily and placed a kiss on my forehead. "Have fun."

Emma spread out the game board, and Derek helped get out the pieces and cards. Collin joined them on the floor cross-legged while chewing on a few pretzels.

"Hey, Kai," Crystal said loud enough for everyone to hear. "That scrapbook you wanted to see is in my room. Want to check it out?"

I took a deep breath and followed her down the

hallway, hoping I'd finally get a chance to learn more about my gift.

8

"Your friends really know what you can do?" I asked as I stepped into her bedroom and out of earshot of the others.

She sat on her bed and nodded.

"So, they're, like, in the loop about what's going on here?"

She nodded again. "I'm sorry. Is that not okay? I didn't tell them what you could do. I just asked them to distract your friends while we talked."

I relaxed the tension in my shoulders I hadn't realized was there and then sank into the chair next to her desk. "No, it's fine. Really."

Crystal shifted on her bed to cross her legs. "So, tell me more about what you can do."

It took me a moment to realize I was chewing my

lower lip. I shrugged. "It's just something I've always been able to do. I don't know; I got lucky, I guess. When I fall asleep, I just get right back up again, only my body doesn't come with me. I look and feel like me, but I can't touch anything. It's like I'm a ghost."

Crystal leaned her chin on her fist like she was invested in my confession. When she didn't say anything, I continued.

"It's kind of like I *am* dreaming. I've never really experienced dreams, but there are similarities from what I've heard."

Crystal tilted her head slightly. "What do you mean by that?"

I pressed my lips together. Admitting all of this felt so strange. I'd never said it all out loud before. "Well, like how you can be in one place one moment and then somewhere else in the blink of an eye. The difference is that it all feels real to me, and I can control where I can go as long as I can visualize it."

"Hmm... So, if it feels real to you, does time move at the same pace?"

I blinked a few times, not sure I understood the question. "What do you mean?"

Crystal dropped her fist from her chin. "Like, for me, time doesn't really apply in my dreams. I could maybe be dreaming just a few minutes and then wake up. Sometimes I might not even remember my dreams. So, I mean, time seems to go faster when I'm sleeping. I mean, it doesn't. It just feels that way."

I nodded. I only understood because of those two weeks where my travels had been replaced by nightmares. "No, it's not like that. I'm aware of everything around me, so if I'm asleep for six hours or something, I experience the full six hours."

Crystal's eyes lit up. "That's cool."

I gave her a nervous smile. "It can get boring sometimes, too. Sometimes I like to just sit there and take in the scene. I play this game with myself where I try to interpret different things around me, like the temperature or the wind."

"You mean you can't feel that kind of stuff?"

I shook my head. "No, but you know how you can feel whatever is happening in your dreams, I mean, to some extent?"

"Mm hmm."

"Well, it's kind of like that. I can feel it because I tell myself to feel it. It just makes sense. But if I'm not paying attention, if my brain doesn't process that I'm supposed to feel something, I don't. Like, if I step into the ocean, it doesn't feel cold because I convince myself it doesn't. I've never actually been to the ocean, so what do I know?"

Crystal smiled. "I think I get what you're saying."

"It'd be so much easier to explain this if I could just bring you along and show you."

The suggestion was in jest, but Crystal's smile grew wider.

"What?" I asked slowly.

She took a second to answer, like she was dragging out the suspense. "Maybe you can. I…um…did leave my body once."

I was practically speechless. "You mean…you can…"

"I don't know." Crystal shrugged off the idea. "It was just the one time. I've been working on it, but I just haven't done it again. But I'm, like, this close." She held her thumb and index finger just millimeters apart.

I raised my brows. "If you really could…I mean, that'd be amazing. I've never seen anyone else astral traveling before."

"I agree," Crystal said. "It would be cool, but I don't know if I can."

"Well, you said you've been practicing. Maybe you'll get it this time."

She sucked in a long breath. "I mean, we could try, but it's the middle of the day. Can you fall asleep now?"

I stood from my chair and walked over to her window. "If we close the blinds and maybe put on some soothing music, I can be out in no time. You?"

She nodded. "Yeah, that's pretty much how I've been practicing relaxation."

I turned back to her after closing the curtains. A small amount of light filled the room just enough that I could still make out shadows of the furniture. "I think it's worth a shot."

The only problem? My heart was pounding so hard that I wasn't sure I could fall asleep. I'd finally found someone who could do what I could! Well, maybe not exactly, but she'd separated her spirit from her body once. It was the closest thing I had to someone like me, and it filled my body with excited nerves.

Crystal tossed a pillow at me, and I situated myself on the floor at the foot of her bed.

She turned to her phone, and a moment later, a slow, melodic tune played through the speakers. She lay on her bed and took a deep breath. "I'll see you on the other side, Kai."

9

As soon as the music began playing, my muscles relaxed. My pounding heart slowed until my nerves finally eased. I took a deep breath in and let it out slowly. Voices echoed down the hall and into the room, but I ignored them and focused instead on the soft melody and my slowing breathing. Though I wasn't tired, it didn't take long for the music to lull me into a light sleep.

My spirit awoke as my body continued to relax. I pushed myself to a standing position and nearly toppled over in response to what I saw. It was like I was seeing doubles. A not-so-solid copy of Crystal's body hovered over her actual body. A strange silver material connected the two copies as if her spirit was made of a million small, shiny strings that tethered her to her body. Her spirit eyes remained closed, like she didn't even realize she'd partially materialized on this plane of existence.

A murmur snapped her spirit back into her body, and she bolted upright in her bed. The motion startled me awake before she could spot me standing there. The image of her sitting in bed washed out of view, and I opened my eyes to the dark ceiling above me.

"Kai," she whispered, peeking her head over the end of the bed. "Are you still awake? It's not working for me."

"You almost did it!" I exclaimed, sitting up.

"I did?" Crystal asked in surprise. "I didn't feel anything."

"It was…really strange. It was like your spirit wanted to separate from your body, but it couldn't quite do it. I've never seen anything like it."

"So, what? I need a nudge into this other plane?"

I nodded. Only, how could we do that? Disappointment washed over me. All my excitement was for nothing. This wasn't going to work.

Crystal's eyes lit up a moment later like she'd had a good idea. "What if you sort of 'pulled' me in?"

I narrowed my eyes in thought. "Is that a thing? Can you do that?"

She let out a light laugh. "I honestly have no idea, but it's worth a shot, right?"

I agreed, but as I lowered myself back to the floor, I had to wonder if we were running out of time. Surely at some point our friends would get bored and come see what we were up to. It wouldn't look like much, but it would wake us up. How long had we been at this anyway?

I tried not to dwell on these thoughts as I once again went through the process of relaxing my body and drifting off into a light sleep. As soon as my body fell asleep, I peeled my spirit away from it and stood. I expected to see the same thing I did before, but instead, I only saw Crystal's solid body lying on her bed. Disappointment hit me again. Had we missed our shot at this?

Just as I formulated the thought, a light silver mist rose from Crystal's body. The threads that appeared to make up her spirit wove together until they began to take the shape of her body. Her features defined until that same copy of her I'd seen before hovered above her sleeping form.

I watched in awe and waited until her spirit had taken full shape—well, as much as it could. It remained slightly transparent, and those silver threads still stretched from her spirit to her body, waving slightly as if a light breeze was traveling through the room.

Pull her in, I thought. I took a deep breath. *Hopefully this works.* I honestly didn't have high hopes.

I reached out toward her spirit's wrist. To my surprise, my hand clamped around something solid. My breath hitched in my throat. It was so strange to *feel* something while outside of my body. Not wanting to waste another second, I gently pulled at Crystal. She felt heavy, like her spirit was resisting and didn't really want to separate from her body just yet. But now that there actually was a smidgen of hope, I couldn't back down. I pulled harder, willing her to join me on this plane.

Please work. Please work. Please work, I chanted in my head.

And then, just like that, Crystal's spirit detached from her body, the silver strings dissipating as if finally giving her permission to join me. Her spirit fell to the ground, and she gazed up at me in shock. "It didn't work?"

I couldn't find my jaw to move my mouth. I was pretty sure it was on the floor right about now, but I was too shocked to go searching for it. All I could do was point to her unmoving form on the bed.

Crystal's eyes shifted to follow my gaze, and she gasped. When she finally found her voice again, she couldn't contain herself. She shot up to stand next to me, never taking her eyes off her body. "It *did* work! This is so cool! It's like looking at myself in a mirror, only *way* freakier. Wow! Think of the things we could do, the people we could help by going unnoticed."

She continued rambling in amazement, but I couldn't process what she was saying when guilt suddenly hit me. Crystal discovers she can do this, and her first reaction is *let's help people*? The more I learned about astral traveling, the more I used it to benefit *me*.

Why couldn't I see the good in the world like she did? Why hadn't I ever realized I could practically be a super hero if I wanted to be?

"You know what else we could do?" Crystal continued. "You said you can go anywhere, right? So, you could, like, come here and pull me out of my body every night so we could go on adventures together! Oh, it would be so fun!"

Crystal's hand grazed my shoulder as she threw her arms out in excitement. The sensation caught me off guard and pulled my full attention back to her. My whole life I'd been able to astral travel, and even though I'd learned a lot about it over the years, there was one thing that remained consistent: I could never touch anything while in my spirit form.

I reached out for Crystal's hand without really deciding to. She eyed me as if to ask what I was doing.

"Feel this?" I asked, squeezing her hand slightly.

She nodded.

"Now try to touch something else. Anything."

"Uh, okay." She turned from me and reached for a stuffed owl sitting on her nightstand. As I expected, her fingers fell straight through it. She took a step back. "Whoa. That is freaky."

I shrugged. I'd always been used to it, but this whole feeling something else while astral traveling was bizarre.

Crystal turned back to me. "So, we can't touch anything here?"

"Apparently just each other."

She nodded like she understood. "So, if we can't touch anything, then why don't we just fall through the floor?"

"Ah, good question, my young grasshopper."

She stifled a laugh while I attempted to suppress my smile.

"Watch this." I plopped myself down at the end of her bed. "Seems pretty solid, right?" I didn't wait for an answer. "But see what happens when I try to grab your blanket?" I demonstrated for her, but my attempts fell flat. I couldn't influence the sheets one bit.

"I don't get it," she told me.

"Right?" I agreed. "I think it has to do with our perception. Like, we're not really standing on the ground or sitting on the bed. We just *think* we are because we tell ourselves we are. Remember how I explained that I can feel the wind if I tell myself I should?"

"Right. So, why do our hands fall through objects? Like, why don't they just slam into something hard? We know the object is there, but we can't influence it." She tried again at the stuffed owl.

"Good question. I think it's because deep down we know that we're not solid but that the stuff around us is. So when you realize that you can't feel or influence the object, the logical explanation then would be because *you're* the thing that's out of place. The difference is that when you walk across the floor, you're not trying to influence it, so nothing is *wrong* about that scenario that you have to make up for. And it's not like you really *feel* the floor under your feet. Make sense?"

Crystal shifted her weight between her feet, perhaps testing my theory. "I guess it kind of makes sense."

"Hey," I joked. "Why am I the one answering all the questions? I came to you so *you* could answer my questions."

She laughed. "I'm not sure how much I can help. You clearly know a lot more about this than I do. Hey! You know what would be fun?"

"Pretending we're ghosts and spying on our friends in the living room?"

A mischievous grin spread across her face. "Kai, I think we are going to get along *very* well."

10

Crystal led the way down the hall. Though I knew our friends wouldn't be able to see or hear us, I still felt the need to remain quiet. By the time we emerged into the living room, Crystal was giggling audibly. I caved and joined in on the laughter.

Crystal knelt next to her friend Derek and cleared her throat. When no one responded, she shot a glance at me. "They really can't see or hear us." She said it like it was a statement, but I could hear the slightest bit of a question behind her tone.

I shook my head. "They really can't."

She waved her hand in front of Derek's face as he took his turn in their game of *Sorry*. Nothing. She did the same thing to her friend Emma. Her attempts couldn't quiet the laughter filling the room.

I stood back with my arms across my chest and observed. Savannah and Emma seemed to be getting along and were laughing about a scene in a movie I hadn't seen yet. Collin and Derek exchanged a few words about the girls' obnoxious behavior. I enjoyed seeing our friends getting along so well, as if they'd known each other forever. Beside them, Crystal continued her way around their small circle, waving her hand in front of each person's face and speaking between their laughter into their ears. A smile of amusement broke across my face as I watched her.

She turned to me again. "This. Is. So. Freaky."

"I know, right?" I couldn't contain the excitement in my voice. I finally had someone to share this with!

"It's like being a ghost," Crystal pointed out while waving her hand in front of Collin's face one last time. Finally, she gave up and turned to me. "It's got to be pretty similar, right? I mean, when I saw you that night, I got this feeling that I always get when ghosts are around."

"Is that what the goosebumps were about?"

"Yeah." She nodded. "Hey, want to get out of here? Our friends are pretty loud."

I glanced back at them. They were now arguing about how many spaces Savannah had taken and if she'd been cheating.

"Sure," I agreed.

I demonstrated for Crystal how easy it was to walk through her front door, and she followed behind me.

"Whoa," Crystal said, staring back at the door. "So weird." She turned back to me. "So, tell me more about what you can do."

I tucked a strand of red hair behind my ear out of habit and led the way down the sidewalk, not really headed in any particular direction. "I don't really know that much. That's why I came here to talk to your mom."

"Honestly, I don't think she knows anything about this stuff, either. She reads tarot cards. That's her thing." She paused for a moment. "Hey, I do have one question. How do we, like, wake up?"

I shrugged but continued walking at a steady pace. "You can just kind of feel that it's time to wake up, and then you do. Isn't that how normal people wake up?"

Crystal squinted into the distance. "I guess."

"Everything around you just disappears, and you wake up back where you fell asleep. You can kind of feel your spirit spring back into your body. You'll see when you wake up."

She bit her lip, but a smile broke out behind the nerves. "It sounds scary! So, what happens to your body while you're out of it?"

I shrugged again. *I don't really know! This is why I need someone who's familiar with this stuff.* "I guess whatever happens when you're asleep. You keep breathing. Your heart keeps beating. Sometimes if you're just on the edge of being awake and asleep, you can hear or feel things around you before you actually wake up. Like, you'll be walking here on the street, and suddenly you feel this warm light weight on you. It's actually your blanket. Or sometimes I hear faint voices of my mom and brother talking in the morning. That's a good indication that you're about to wake up."

Crystal nodded like it all made sense, and then she inhaled a deep breath as if testing the air.

"You can't smell anything," I told her.

"You can just hear and see, then?" she asked, almost in disappointment.

"That's how it works for me, at least. It's kind of like watching something on TV, only you're actually in the scene. Almost like virtual reality, I guess. You can hear and see stuff, but you can't smell or touch or taste anything."

She fell silent for a beat as if digesting the idea. "How'd you figure this all out, that you could do this?"

I kept my eyes locked on the sidewalk in front of us. "It's just something I've always been able to do."

"You think it runs in your family?"

I shook my head.

"Oh, because my gift runs in my family. As you know, my mom's psychic, too. I thought maybe if you're looking for answers, someone in your family might know something."

"Well, I know no one in my immediate family can astral travel. When they talked about their dreams, they always sounded so strange. As you can see, it's a lot like being in your body. It's just that no one can see you, and you can't touch anything." I sighed. "I mean, maybe it came from one of my grandparents, but they're long gone."

My heart dropped when I thought about my grandmother. She'd died only a month after I figured out I could travel anywhere by visualizing my destination.

"It's really strange to finally interact with someone," I admitted. "When I look at you, you seem so solid, like you're actually in your body. It almost makes me wonder if I've seen other astral travelers before but didn't realize it."

Crystal stared into the distance, absorbing the concept. Her posture quickly changed when she came up with another question. "Can you get hurt while outside of your body?"

It took me a moment to formulate a response. "I guess your body could get hurt, just like anyone who's sleeping. But, I mean, your spirit can't get physically hurt." Excitement surged through me when I realized I could finally share one of my stories with someone. "Here's an example. In my town, there's this bluff that I run up to every night. At the top, there's a cliff with a river at the bottom. I always assumed I couldn't get hurt while astral traveling, so I wasn't scared to hang my feet off the edge of the cliff."

"Wait, so you can get hurt?" Crystal asked.

I shot her a sly smile. "Just let me finish. Okay, so I was sitting there in my spirit form with my legs dangling off the edge of the cliff. I got bored, so I started to get up to walk over to a different part of the cliff. Just as I was getting up, this crazy loud owl screeched. I swear it was in the tree next to me. Anyway, I was so startled that I lost my footing, and I *fell*."

Crystal gasped. "You *fell* off the cliff?"

"And this is why I was always scared to get close to the edge in my body. Because as graceful as I may be while running, apparently I suck at standing up." I laughed at myself, but it was more of a nervous giggle.

Crystal turned down a new street, and I followed. "So, what happened when you fell?"

"I woke up." I smiled.

"You just woke up?"

"Oh, don't get me wrong. It was scary as hell. I mean, I felt myself falling. But I guess that made my heart rate spike, and it woke me. So if you really think you're in danger, you'll just wake up."

Crystal pressed her lips together. "Makes sense. But what if, like, your body died while your spirit was outside of it?"

I laughed lightly. "Believe me, I do not want to figure that one out. But you're the expert on ghosts. Don't you think your spirit would just move on or whatever?"

Crystal scoffed. "I wouldn't say expert, but I guess something like that might happen. It'd just be kind of sad if you got stuck here, you know? I'd *hope* you could move on."

"Well, let's also hope that neither of us has to figure

that one out."

She laughed. "Agreed. So, you say you can travel anywhere as long as you can visualize it?"

I nodded.

She stared up at the sky. "Could you go to the moon?"

"You're bold," I said bluntly, raising my brows.

She pushed blond hair out of her face and laughed. "I don't know about that."

"I honestly have never tried it," I told her. "As far as I know, it would work. I've never been limited by where I could go. I just haven't had the balls to try it yet."

"What's the worst that could happen? You'd just wake up, right?"

"I guess so, but you know what? I have so much of the world left to see that I haven't even really thought about visiting the stars."

Silence stretched between us for several seconds while Crystal thought my answer over. She was the first to break the silence. "How did you learn to do it? To go somewhere else, I mean."

"It was just a fluke thing," I said. "I was 12 when I heard my parents talking about their divorce. I was astral traveling at the time. I just wanted to get away from it and go to my grandma's, and so I closed my eyes and visualized her house. When I opened them, I was there." I shrugged like it was simple.

"It's just that easy?" Crystal asked. "Just close your

eyes and visualize a place? That's it?"

"Well, not always," I laughed. "At first, it didn't always work. I'd be standing in my bedroom and close my eyes and visualize a place, and when I opened them, I was still in my room. Or sometimes I'd be thinking of a place when another one would pop into my mind, and I'd end up there instead. It took several months before I trained my mind to focus enough that it came easily to me. I think it worked the first time because my emotions were so high, you know?"

Crystal twisted her mouth to the side like she was nervous.

"What is it?" I asked.

She slowed her pace. "I practice a lot with focusing my mind to improve my abilities. Do you think I have what it takes to do it?"

"Yeah. Where do you want to go?"

We stopped in the middle of the sidewalk and turned to each other.

She took a deep breath while thinking of her destination. "Why don't we start out with something easy? Something close by and familiar? What about my mom's shop?"

"Sure," I agreed.

"Okay, um." Crystal twisted her hands around each other. "Can you hold my hand? I—I know that sounds silly, but I thought that maybe it would help like how you pulled me in before."

"Of course." I reached out for her hand. Again, it hit

me how odd it felt to touch something solid while I was outside my body. "Ready?"

She closed her eyes and drew in a long breath. "Ready."

11

I closed my eyes with her and visualized her mom's shop. When I opened them, we were both there, our hands still locked together. Sunlight spilled in through the display windows to light up the shop. Colors of all shades hit my senses, from the rainbow of candles on the table to our right to the dream catchers across the room. Quiet, peaceful music that I hadn't noticed before played softly in the background.

When my eyes fell on Crystal next to me, hers were still squeezed tightly shut. I gently tightened my grip on her hand to get her attention. "You can open your eyes now."

When she did, a look of wonder filled them. She didn't say anything, but that shock in her eyes was all too familiar to me.

"Uh oh!" Crystal's stance changed, catching me off guard. She planted her feet firmly on the ground like she was trying to keep her balance. "Do you feel that?"

I stood still in shock, wondering what could possibly be happening. Was she having some sort of reaction to traveling?

"What is it?" I asked with concern.

She blinked a few times. "I—I think I'm waking up."

A split second later, she vanished before my eyes. It was like someone had flipped a switch on her existence. At first, a jolt of fear surged through me. I'd never traveled with anyone before, and of course, I didn't know what it looked like when *I* returned to my body. Witnessing it happen to someone else was an entirely new experience for me—and a freaky one at that.

I forced myself to calm down. *She just woke up. That's it. Now you wake up.* I wasn't in a deep sleep, so I found my eyes with ease. When I opened them, I was back in Crystal's room in my own body.

Crystal popped her head over the side of the bed again. "Of all the things I can do, I have to say that astral traveling is one of the coolest!"

I pushed myself to a sitting position and crossed my legs, facing Crystal. I wasn't sure what woke her, but I was happy to hear that our friends were still laughing in the living room and not bothering us.

"I'm glad you're having so much fun with it," I told her. I didn't voice my true thoughts, though. *I'm happy I finally have someone to share this with.*

Why is it then that I feel so bad about it? I wondered.

I wasn't even sure what I was feeling. Guilt, perhaps? It was only when I honed my attention on Savannah's voice from the living room that I realized what was bothering me. If I became friends with Crystal, it was almost like I was *cheating* on Savannah. She was my best friend, and as BFF's, we had a duty to tell each other everything. Yet here I was sharing my deepest darkest secret with a complete stranger, and I couldn't even tell Savannah? It didn't seem fair to her.

Collin's voice echoed down the hall, and a second wave of guilt hit me. If I was going to start telling people about what I could do, I should at least tell my boyfriend, right? I mean, we hadn't been going out that long, but I trusted him wholeheartedly.

"What's wrong?" Crystal asked after a stretch of silence.

Apparently my discomfort was written on my face. Usually I was good at hiding that.

I swallowed hard before answering her. Why was it so easy to open up to her anyway? "I'm just thinking about telling my friends. It honestly doesn't seem fair that I told you about what I can do before I told them. No offense."

"None taken." She shifted to cross her legs on the bed.

"How did you —" I paused for a moment, unsure of how to word the question. "How did you tell your friends? I mean, they all know, right?"

She nodded and shrugged at the same time. "I just told them flat out. I mean, they needed some convincing, but they're my friends. We trust each other. I would think your friends would trust you, too."

I tried not to let my uncertainty bleed into my tone. "They do trust me, but we've never talked about this kind of stuff, the paranormal or whatever. I worry that they'll think I'm playing a trick on them or something."

"Do you think it'd help if I was there?" she asked.

I shifted uncomfortably. It might be easier with her there, but she was still a stranger. I wasn't sure if having her there during such a huge moment in my life was what I wanted. Still, I had *astral traveled* with her. That had to count for something, right?

"I'm not even sure if I'll tell them, to be honest," I finally said. "Savannah and I have been friends as long as I can remember. I've never said anything about it before. It almost seems a little too late to say anything now."

A look of uncertainty crossed Crystal's face, but she simply said, "Well, if you do need help telling them, you can count on me."

I gazed up at her sheepishly. "Thanks."

A moment of silence fell over the room, and an awkward energy sizzled between us. To ease the silence, I spoke. "Want to go see what they're doing out there?" I gestured toward the living room. "Maybe we can get in on their next game."

"Sure," she agreed, hoping off the bed.

When Crystal and I entered the living room, I sank down next to Collin. He automatically took my hand in his.

"Oh, great!" Emma said excitedly as Crystal squeezed into the circle we formed. "You guys are just in time. We were going to pull out a new game. What do you think? Cranium?"

While Emma, Savannah, and Crystal discussed the next game, Collin leaned into me and spoke quietly.

"What have you two been up to?"

The question was only out of genuine curiosity. He deserved some sort of answer, but he wouldn't understand the truth.

I simply shrugged and said, "Nothing."

"Come on." He nudged me with his shoulder. "You know you can tell me anything."

My cheeks began to heat, and I knew it showed on my face. "We just talked," I told him.

Collin leaned away from me and released my hand. Thank goodness he stopped pushing it! I wasn't ready to tell him about my gift yet. I wasn't sure I'd ever be ready.

"Okay, we'll do three teams," Emma said before splitting us into groups of two.

12

"What game do you want to play next?" Emma asked excitedly after we finished our game of Cranium, which she and Derek won.

A knot formed in my stomach. I honestly didn't want to play anything. I wanted to talk to Crystal's mom, and I mentally kicked myself for not taking the chance to meet her earlier while we were at the shop. *Not another game. Not another game,* I chanted in my head. I released the breath I was holding when Collin came to my rescue, not that he picked up on my silent plea, but it was better than nothing.

"I'm actually pretty hungry," he said. "Is there anywhere to eat in this town?"

Emma crinkled her nose in thought, which made her look an awful lot like a chipmunk. "We have a little café."

"I'm hungry, too," Savannah agreed. "We should all go get something together."

Emma exchanged a glance with Derek the same time Crystal gazed in my direction as if we are all gauging each other's thoughts.

"Sounds good," Emma agreed.

"We'll have to take two cars," Collin pointed out.

Crystal shrugged. "Or we can walk. It's really not that far."

The knot in my gut tightened. I had to suggest meeting Crystal's mom at some point before my friends got bored enough to insist we leave. Only, the idea of bringing up the topic sent nerves racing through my body.

"Hey, Crystal." I cleared my throat before anyone could stand and prepare to leave. "Didn't your mom want to meet me before I left town?"

She caught on to my hint quickly. "You're right. She did want to meet you." She glanced between her friends. "How about Kai and I stop by the shop for a couple of minutes? You can order me a burger, and we'll be at the café by the time the food gets there." She looked back to me. "What do you want?"

I shrugged. "A burger sounds fine."

"Okay." Crystal pushed herself up from the floor. "Kai and I will meet you guys at the café in a bit."

The rest of us stood. As the girls shuffled around for their shoes and purses, Collin gripped my hand and leaned into me. "I can come with you, too."

"It's okay, really." I gave him a smile as reassurance. *Please don't come with*, I prayed. I wouldn't be able to ask any questions about my gift if he did. "I'm having fun getting to know Crystal."

"Well, what if I want to get to know her, too? I like running, you know."

At first, I didn't understand why he was pointing out the obvious. What did running have to do with being friends with Crystal? *Right.* I'd told him we became friends over our mutual love of running.

"But then Savannah would be all alone." I glanced over at her. She laughed at something Emma said while she flipped her purple hair and slung her purse across her shoulder.

Collin followed my gaze. I didn't miss the fallen expression that crossed his face for a moment. "Okay," he finally said. "I'll see you in a bit." He placed a kiss on the top of my forehead before turning to follow Savannah out the door.

Crystal and I walked with them for two blocks and then went a separate way to detour to Divination.

"So, what kind of questions will you ask my mom?" she asked.

Though I burned with curiosity about my gift, I honestly didn't know.

***

By the time we emerged from the shop, I hadn't learned anything new about astral traveling. For being a supernatural guru, Crystal's mom really didn't seem to know much—at least, nothing that could help me.

"Astral traveling?" she'd asked curiously. "I've heard of it but never met anyone who could do it." She'd leaned her elbow up against the break room table the three of us sat around. "Tell me more about what that's like."

I ended up answering more questions than I'd asked.

"I'm sorry my mom couldn't help you," Crystal said on our walk to the café.

I crossed my arms over my chest to keep my body heat close to my core. "It's not a big deal," I told her, but I was lying. Luckily, I was a pretty good liar.

"You know what, though?" She gazed at me while we walked. "I don't think you need as much help as you think you do."

Finally, I tore my gaze from the sidewalk and met her eyes. "What do you mean?"

"My mom and I asked a lot of questions about your gift. Not *one* of those questions stumped you. And let's be honest, you didn't really ask any questions of your own."

"Yes I did," I insisted.

Only, looking back on it, I realized I hadn't been asking questions. At first, I thought it was because they were asking so many of me that I couldn't get my own questions in. But now that Crystal pointed it out, it was because I didn't know what to ask. My questions had been pretty limited to, "Do you know anything about astral traveling?" and "Can you tell me more about it?" But I wasn't even curious about the specifics. Was that because I'd already learned what I needed to on my own? I'd come to Peyton Springs wondering one thing: were there other people out there like me? Not only did I get an answer to that question, but I *met* someone else who was like me—on some level, at least.

Realizing that I'd accomplished what I came here for sent a wave of relief throughout my body. All I needed to know was that I wasn't alone in this.

"I guess you're right, Crystal," I finally said. "I got the help I needed today."

13

Crystal and I entered the café right on time. Just as we slid into chairs next to our friends, the waitress arrived with our meals.

"Perfect timing," Derek said, smiling.

"Did you have fun?" Collin asked, leaning into my left shoulder.

"It was okay. I just said hi to Crystal's mom and she asked me a couple of questions, and that was it." At least it was the truth, and it sounded innocent enough.

Collin bit into a fry, but he didn't take his eyes off me. Once he swallowed, he spoke again in a low voice. The other conversations around the table drowned out his question so that only I could hear.

"What's up with you, Kai?" he asked. It almost sounded like he was *accusing* me of something.

"Up with me?" I asked innocently as I squirted a mountain of ketchup onto my plate. "Nothing's up with me."

He leaned in even closer to whisper in my ear. "You're a dirty little liar."

The words were meant as a playful jab, but my entire body froze, and a chill ran down my spine.

"Wh—what would make you say that?" I silently cursed myself for letting my voice waver.

He placed another fry in his mouth. "You haven't been yourself all day."

I shrugged and bit into my burger like that would somehow hide my anxiety. *Normally I'm good at this. Why do I suck so badly today?*

"I was just nervous about meeting Crystal." I didn't bother swallowing first. Maybe if I spoke while chewing, he couldn't tell how nervous he was making me. I *so* wasn't ready to tell him about my gift yet.

Crystal burst into laughter across the table, pulling my attention from Collin. I wasn't sure what someone had said to make her laugh, but now Emma, Derek, and Savannah were laughing, too. My gaze locked across the table at Crystal and her friends. If she could tell them about what she could do and they accepted that and still had so much fun with her, couldn't I muster up the same level of courage?

No, I can't, I told myself.

But you should, another voice countered. *It's never going to be the right time to tell them, and at some point, it will be too late.*

"Are you even listening to me?" Collin's voice pulled me from my thoughts.

"What?" I turned to him and blinked a few times. I had to think back on what he was just saying, and bits and pieces of it began to process in my mind. "Yeah, you were saying that I wasn't acting like myself all day."

His gaze fell to his plate, and he spoke softly, so softly that I hardly heard him above the other chatter at the table. "It's like you're keeping something from me." He cleared his throat and gently wiped his mouth with his napkin. "Excuse me."

I swore that as he stood and retreated from our table, my heart dropped out of my chest and onto the floor. It was evident in his tone that he was upset with me, and I wasn't prepared to handle that. I stared after him for so long that even after he disappeared down the hall that led to the restrooms, I hadn't noticed the silence that had settled over our table. Finally, I turned back to everyone else. They all stared at me, and my whole body tensed.

"What was that about?" Savannah asked. "Are you two good?"

I shrugged and dipped a fry into my ketchup. "I'm not sure. I guess he's mad at me."

"What for?" Crystal asked, but I had a feeling she already knew on some level.

I couldn't bring myself to eat the fry.

"Do you want me to go check on him?" Derek

offered.

I dropped the fry onto my plate. I understood why he was offering since Collin had just gone to the men's restroom, but it didn't seem right to ask a stranger to fight my battles for me.

"No," I answered with a surprising edge of confidence to my voice. "I'll go see if he's okay." I pushed my chair away from the table and stood on shaky legs. *This could be it*, I told myself. It made me want to run back to my friends and hide under the table, but I pushed forward toward the restrooms. I knocked lightly on the men's room door and called out. "Collin, are you okay?"

No answer came. *Maybe he didn't go to the bathroom,* I theorized. I glanced around in search of another door. The only other two places he could have gone were to the ladies' room or the kitchen. Clearly the men's room was the best bet. I almost considered peeking my head in to make sure, but before I could honestly consider that idea, the door creaked open.

I didn't let him get a word out before I spoke. "You're mad at me." It wasn't a question.

He sighed and opened the door further, emerging into the secluded hallway. "It's just that you seem to be hiding something from me."

My jaw hung open. *Say something, you fool!* I told myself. Only, I couldn't find the words.

"It's not just today." Collin crossed his arms and leaned his back against the wall but kept his gaze locked on the tile floor. "It's like this whole time we've been going out you've been wanting to tell me something but won't."

I recalled the day he asked me about it when we went running together. How was it that I'd been able to keep this secret from everyone I knew for the last 16 years, yet in the first month we start dating he'd picked up on my lies? He believed all my other lies. I thought I could play my way through this one, too.

"It's unfair," he muttered so softly that I barely heard him.

"What's unfair?" I asked.

He shrugged and looked toward the opposite end of the hall. It was like I wasn't supposed to hear him say that, like he wasn't willing to explain. I dared to step closer to him, but the thought of reaching out to comfort him only broke my heart further. He was really hurting here, and it was all because of me. Heat rose to my cheeks as that sense of guilt I'd been feeling so much lately burrowed deeper into the pit of my stomach.

Collin caved. "It's just that I opened up to you even before we were dating. I have *always* been unfairly forgiving toward you. I went along with everything you said, every suggestion you had, when we were looking into my sister's murder. I didn't need an explanation. I just *trusted* you." He raked his fingers through his hair before finishing in a near whisper. "Why can't you trust me, too?"

"Collin." This time I reached out to touch him. It

was just a light caress of his arm, but it was enough to show I cared. "I *do* trust you."

"Then why can't you tell me about whatever it is you've been worrying about? I want to be there for you. I want to help."

He surprised me by uncrossing his arms and pulling me into a hug. His breath warmed the upper half of my face. I completely relaxed into his embrace. It was as if he had the power to mend my heart and ease that knot in my gut. Neither of us said anything for nearly a minute. We simply stood there holding each other, soothing each other. It gave me the time to reflect on all of this. What was I waiting for anyway? Why hadn't I told anyone before? I told Crystal, and that wasn't so bad. Her friends knew about her, and they didn't lock her up in a mental institution. It couldn't be so bad to tell my friends, could it?

When I finally pulled away from him and looked into his eyes, I was filled with a new-found confidence. Ever since I'd lost my gift for a brief period last month, I'd been thinking more and more about telling someone about it, about telling my best friends. Why wait any longer?

"Okay, Collin. I'll tell you."

14

I took Collin's hand and led him back to our table. Savannah eyed us curiously but finally broke her stare once we sat down. The legs of my chair screeched as I scooted myself closer to the table. My gaze traveled toward Crystal across from me in hopes that she could somehow help me find the courage to do this. She smiled back reassuringly. *If she can do this,* I thought, *so can I.*

I sipped my water and cleared my throat. Silence had settled over the table as if everyone expected me to break it. *You can do this, Kai.*

"I, um, have something to tell you guys." I faced my two best friends and ignored Crystal's friends even though they seemed interested as well. Unlike my friends, though, they continued eating. For some reason, having them nearby gave me even more confidence. I mean, I never thought when I told my friends that I'd do it in front of strangers, but it helped to know that Crystal's friends believed her and at least some people at the table would believe me, too.

Savannah raised her eyebrows in interest, but I couldn't read Collin's expression. Another glance in Crystal's direction, and I knew I couldn't stall any longer. I had to do this. If I was going to share this with anyone, I wanted my best friends to be a part of it.

"There's, uh, no easy way to say this. You probably won't believe me anyway." I forced my hands between my shaking knees to keep the nerves at bay. It didn't work. "I have a gift. I never told anyone about it…until today. And I think you guys deserve to know, too."

Collin and Savannah narrowed their eyes subtly, but no one spoke. It was like they were giving me a chance to spit it out at my own pace. Only, I didn't know how to say it. *What had I said to Crystal earlier today to make her believe me?*

"I guess I, um… Here's the thing… I've never asked either of you before what you thought of the paranormal, like ghosts and psychics and whatever. Every time the subject comes up, I avoid it. It's because, well, I *do* believe in that kind of stuff. And the thing is, I can do it."

I tried to gauge my friends' reactions, but their expressions remained blank.

Finally, Savannah spoke. "You've completely lost

me, Kai. Are you trying to tell us you're Wiccan or something?"

"What? No. I—"

"Maybe I can help," Crystal offered.

"Crystal," I began to say under my breath, but she stopped me.

"It's okay," she told me. "I'm not shy about it, not anymore." She turned back to my friends. "I'm psychic. I can see ghosts and predict future events and sometimes see people's memories. I can also find things. I can't do most of it on demand, but the fact is that I'm *different* from most people."

Collin let out a light laugh. "You're not serious."

Crystal's expression didn't shift. "I am. And Kai…"

"I'm different, too," I interrupted. I needed them to hear this from me. Saying it out loud felt like a massive weight had been lifted off my shoulders. All this time I'd been keeping this to myself, and it had built tension inside of me I hadn't realized was there until I finally spilled the secret.

"What do you mean, you're different?" Collin asked.

"I don't get it," Savannah said at the same time.

I sighed. Had it been this hard for Crystal to tell her friends?

Emma cut in with a confident voice. "I can vouch for them." She straightened in her seat. "You see, everyone is born with a level of intuition. Some people, like Crystal, are born with a more natural connection to the other side. Kai is the same way. Well, I assume." She looked to me for confirmation. "What is it you can do, anyway?"

"Wait. Hold on," Savannah insisted. "Kai, you're saying you're *psychic*?"

"No, I—" I started, but Collin's voice cut me off.

"It's not very nice to play games with us when we're only trying to help."

With that, tears began to well in my eyes. How could he not see I was being serious? Luckily, Crystal and her friends all came to my rescue at the same time, including Derek, who had remained pretty shy up to this point. They all rambled simultaneously, and I couldn't focus on one voice over the others.

"Just hold up." Collin held his hands out to calm everyone. Once the table went quiet again, he turned to me. "You mean, you actually believe in this stuff?"

My head shook ever so slightly. "It's not about *believing* it. I *know* it." And that's when I realized for the first time that those words were true. I'd never told anyone before because I never *truly* knew I wasn't crazy. But after everything that happened last month, there was no doubt about it. My travels weren't a figment of my imagination. And Crystal helped confirm that enough so that there wasn't the slightest doubt in my mind.

As soon as this realization struck, the words tumbled out of me. He *had* to believe me. "Every night when I fall asleep, my spirit separates from my body. I can go anywhere I want, see anything in real time. My body sleeps, but my spirit stays awake, roaming a different place each night until I wake again and my spirit reunites with my body. It's something I've always been able to do. I don't know why I was given this gift, but I *do* know I'm not the only one who can do it." I glanced toward Crystal, who was smiling proudly.

When I looked back to Collin, I grabbed his hand, willing him to believe me. "I also know that I can't keep this to myself any longer. I *hate* lying to you guys." My face heated, and my voice came out small. "I don't want to be alone anymore." A tear rolled down my face.

"It's just so…" Collin's voice trailed off.

Savannah finished his sentence for him. "Unbelievable."

A nervous giggle escaped my lips. "I know."

"Maybe we can prove it to you," Emma offered.

I shot her a smile as a thank you.

"You know, I didn't believe it for a long time, either," Derek said, resting his elbows on the table. "I was skeptical until…well…" He glanced between the two girls beside him. "Until something happened to me."

"Something happened to you?" Savannah leaned into the table in interest.

"No offense," Collin said, "but we don't really know you, any of you. I'm not saying you're not trustworthy, but how can we know you guys aren't all in on the joke?"

"Well, you're considering it, aren't you?" Emma challenged.

"Collin," I said, squeezing his hand tighter while wiping away the tears with the other. "It's not a joke. Really." Once again, I looked to Crystal for help.

"I don't like running," she blurted.

A look of confusion crossed everyone's faces.

"I mean, that's not why Kai came here," Crystal clarified. "I didn't even know her before today."

"She's right," I said, turning back to my friends. "I lied to you about us meeting online because I was afraid to tell you about what I could do. I wanted to come here to ask Crystal questions about it." A long pause finally allowed a moment for me to inhale a deep breath.

"I don't get it," Savannah said for the umpteenth time. "If you've always been able to do this, why hasn't it ever come up before? Why haven't you ever said anything?"

Hot tears rose to my eyes again, and my voice cracked. "I was afraid you'd think I was crazy."

As soon as the tears began running down my cheeks again, a frown formed across Savannah's face. She stood and rounded Collin's chair to wrap her arms around me. "Oh, Kai. I'd never call you crazy." She pulled away to look me in the eyes. "Besides, I'm a little crazy myself." She rolled her eyes and pointed to her purple hair as if that was proof of her insanity. "They'd never get you out of Amberg without hauling me along with you to the looney bin."

I couldn't help the genuine laughter that erupted out of my lungs. Once I managed to calm down, I wiped the tears from my eyes. "Thanks, Savannah."

She retreated to her seat while I turned to Collin. His expression remained neutral. I had no idea what he was thinking.

As I tried to come up with an answer, he surprised me by pulling me into a hug. After placing a kiss on the top of my head, he said, "Thank you for being honest with me."

I couldn't tell if he believed me or was just going along with it for my sake, but I wasn't sure that mattered. I had what I needed: his support.

15

The whole ride home consisted of me answering Savannah's unending stream of questions about my gift. I managed to come clean to my friends about everything, including about how my astral travels played a role in solving Collin's sister's murder.

My heart broke a little the farther we drove from Peyton Springs. I had really made a friend in Crystal today, and I wanted to get to know her better. I relaxed a little when I realized I'd have plenty of time to do that later tonight.

By the time Savannah dropped me off at home, darkness had settled over Amberg. The porch light was on as if my mom was waiting for me. I quickly checked my phone but found no text or missed call from her.

"Okay," I said, slipping my phone back into my

pocket. "I'll see you guys on Monday."

"Bye, Kai." Savanah waved from the driver's seat. "Sleep tight."

I laughed lightly and then turned to Collin. He pulled me into a hug and placed a light kiss on my lips.

"I'm glad you opened up to us," he said.

"I'm just glad you guys didn't freak. You're both the best." I threw my arms around his neck and squeezed him tightly. Then I gave Savannah a wave and stepped out of the car.

The front door seemed distant. I inhaled a deep breath, and somehow, that made it seem within reach. *Let's get this over with.*

When I walked through the door, the scent of tomatoes and chili powder hit my nose. I crossed the living room and entered the kitchen to find my mom standing at the stove.

"You're making chili?" I asked.

She turned to me with a smile.

"*We're* making chili," my brother's voice corrected. He stepped out from behind the pantry door with a bag of noodles in his hand.

"Noodles in chili?" I asked. *Weird.*

"It's what the recipe calls for," he sneered, pointing his tongue in my direction. That used to be a sign that he basically despised me; now it was just a teasing gesture.

I stepped around the counter. "Do you need any help?"

"Could you set the table?" my mom asked.

"Sure."

I moved to the cupboards to pull out three bowls and spoons, but my hands shook slightly. I had to tell my family what I could do, and I wasn't sure how. I didn't have Crystal, Emma, and Derek to back me up this time. I waited until we were all seated around the table and had dished up our chili. After a bite, I realized the noodles weren't that bad in it. I couldn't bring myself to take another scoop, though. I had to tell them first.

"Mom. Braden. I have something to tell you guys."

My eyes remained locked on my bowl of chili, but I could see their expressions of curiosity out of the corner of my eye. Lifting my gaze, I suddenly became filled with a sense of confidence. I decided there was no point in stalling, so I spoke before either of them could prod me to continue.

"I have this gift. It's called astral traveling or astral projection. Basically, when I fall asleep, my spirit leaves my body. I can travel the world in real-time. I don't know why I have this gift since it doesn't seem to run in the family." I shrugged. "I guess some people are just more connected to things like this than others. I've always been able to do it, and I just wanted you guys to know. I don't want to hide who I am anymore."

I didn't know what I was expecting from my family, but it didn't surprise me when Braden burst into a laughing fit and my mother raised her eyebrows and nodded her head slowly.

"Okay, honey," she said as if I was a child who told her I'd seen the tooth fairy.

"Good one, Kai," Braden laughed before shoveling another two spoonfuls of chili in his mouth.

A grin broke out across my face. It didn't matter if they believed me. All that mattered was that my secret was now out in the open. And that left me feeling more confident than I'd ever felt before.

***

After brushing my teeth and slipping into my pajamas that night, I crossed the hall and knocked on my mother's bedroom door. As long as I was spilling secrets, I might as well ease my guilt about disobeying her.

"Come in," she called.

I stepped into her room to see she was propped up on her bed working on something on her computer. She looked up at me and set the laptop aside. I crossed the room and took a seat next to her on the bed.

"What is it, Kai?" she asked.

I cleared my throat. "Mom, I did something that you're not going to be happy about."

She raised her brows questioningly.

I inched closer to her on the bed. "I, um, went and visited my friend even when you said I couldn't."

"You *what*?" she practically shouted, sitting up

straighter in the bed.

"I went and visited my friend even though—"

"I heard you the first time," she interrupted. Then to my surprise, she began laughing. I didn't know what to do when she reached out to me as if she wanted to pull me into an embrace. Though confusion had settled over me, I crawled across the bed and into her arms. She wrapped them around me in a warm, comforting hug.

"Oh, honey," she laughed. "I'm just glad you're okay."

"You mean, you're not mad at me?" I asked in shock.

"Don't get me wrong. You're grounded for a week. I'm just so happy to see that I raised an honest child."

I never expected anyone to call me *honest* given how often I lied, but another surge of confidence hit me when I heard my mother say those words.

"I'm reducing your grounding sentence from a month down to a week for being honest," she joked with a laugh.

"Good to know being honest pays off," I joked back.

"I can't go *that* easy on you. After all the chores I have planned for you, you'll never disobey me again."

Her tone implied she was kidding, but I knew she was dead serious. I'd be spending the next week scrubbing toilets and cleaning baseboards until they were so spotless even Mr. Clean would be impressed. I totally deserved it, but meeting Crystal was worth it.

My mom pulled away from me, and her expression

turned serious. "Really, Kai. I'm just glad you're okay." The touching moment only lasted for a second before she turned back to her half joking mode. "Now go get some sleep. You're going to need to be in peak condition tomorrow for all the cleaning you have ahead of you."

"Ha ha," I said dryly.

"You know I'm serious," she said as I crossed the room.

"I know," I called back before closing the door. "The joke's on you, though. I *love* cleaning."

She raised her voice as I shut the door. "Fine by me."

"As long as we're being honest," I shouted on my way back to my room, "I was lying. Cleaning *sucks*."

Her laughter faded once I shut my bedroom door. I didn't even care about my punishment. Nothing could kill the smile on my face that formed when I realized that for *once* my mom and I were actually getting along.

I crawled into bed, closed my eyes, and waited patiently for my astral travels to whisk me away on another adventure.

ABOUT THE AUTHOR

Alicia Rades is a USA Today bestselling author of young adult paranormal fiction with a love for supernatural stories set in the modern world. When she's not plotting out fiction novels, you can find her writing content for various websites or plowing her way through her never-ending reading list. Alicia holds a bachelor's degree in communications with an emphasis on professional writing.

CPSIA information can be obtained
at www.ICGtesting.com
Printed in the USA
FSHW021049211118
53958FS